Spider Storch's
Carpool
Catastrophe

Gina Willner-Pardo
illustrated by Nick Sharratt

A TRUMPET CLUB SPECIAL EDITION

ISBN 0-590-70633-0

Text copyright © 1997 by Gina Willner-Pardo.
Illustrations copyright © 1997 by Nick Sharratt. All rights reserved.
Published by Scholastic Inc., 555 Broadway, New York, NY 10012,
by arrangement with Albert Whitman & Company.
TRUMPET and associated logos are trademarks and/or registered
trademarks of Scholastic Inc.

12 11 10 9 8 7 6 5 4 3 2 1   8 9/9 0 1 2 3/0

Printed in the U.S.A.   40

First Scholastic printing, September 1998

Designed by Scott Piehl.

For Cara, who is totally cool about
spiders and everything else.
—G. W.-P.

For Edgar and Roman.
—N. S.

Don't forget to read...

Spider Storch's
Teacher Torture

by Gina Willner-Pardo

illustrated by Nick Sharratt

Contents

1

Mom's New Friend

"Joey Storch! Will you answer me, please?" Mom said.

Mom refused to call me Spider, which is what my friends call me.

"What?" I said, looking up from my book. I was studying a picture of a raft spider and trying to see the claws at the end of its feet.

"Guess who I saw at the gym?"

"Who?"

"Diane Brennerman," Mom said.

Mary Grace Brennerman is in my third grade. Once I tried to light her hair on fire. I didn't know any Diane Brennerman.

"Does Mary Grace have a sister?" I asked.

Mom smiled. "Diane Brennerman is Mary Grace's *mother*."

"Oh," I said.

"We got to talking on the exercise bikes," Mom said. "She knows the Hallenbecks."

"No kidding," Dad said. "Small world."

"She's quite a cook, evidently. She told me about an advanced class in Italian cooking at the community center," Mom said. "I really like her."

"Ooh," my sister, Louise, said. "Maybe Mom and Mrs. Brennerman can get you and Mary Grace together for play dates." Louise was lying on the floor. She is eleven. She is 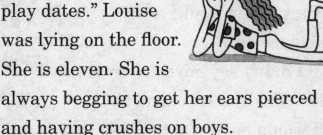 always begging to get her ears pierced and having crushes on boys.

"Quit it," I said.

"We were thinking of carpooling to school and back," Mom said. "It's silly for both of us to do all that driving."

"You mean I'd have to go to school with Mary Grace?"

"Mm-hm."

"And come home?"

"Yeah." Mom gave me a big smile from her corner of the couch.

"You mean I'd have to ride in the same car with her?" I shrieked.

"Come on, Joey," Mom said. She sat forward. "Carpooling would really help me out."

I didn't say anything more. I'm usually a lot of trouble. It would be nice to help her out for a change.

"You and Mary Grace might get to be friends," Mom said. "You never know."

Mom is always saying "you never know."

I did so know. Just the idea of breathing the same car air as Mary Grace Brennerman made me want to throw up.

2

Rotten Mary Grace

Mary Grace Brennerman tells on you for things like whispering during filmstrips or sneezing and then wiping your hand on your pants. She is always reminding the teacher which kid has to go to Speech and volunteering to erase the blackboard. I have known her since kindergarten. Even in kindergarten, she was rotten.

"I can't believe you have to ride to school with her," Zachary said the next morning at the playground.

"What if people see you both getting out of the same car?" Andrew said.

I nodded. "It's only October and the whole year's already ruined."

"Uh-oh, Spider," Zachary whispered. "Look who's coming."

Mary Grace was walking right toward us. Her ponytail bounced around on her head. She looked like she was smelling something bad.

"Why are you all red?" she asked when she got close. She looked disgusted. Mary Grace can't stand it when boys get sweaty.

"I was playing," I said.

"You weren't running in the halls,

were you?" Mary Grace asked. "Because you're not supposed to run in the halls."

"I wasn't in the halls," I said. "I was playing. I just said."

With Mary Grace, you're always explaining things, even when they aren't any of her business.

"You weren't playing with spiders again, were you?" she asked.

I sighed. "No."

"Because spiders can be dangerous," Mary Grace said. "Black widows can kill you."

Mary Grace always thinks she knows everything.

"Black widows almost never bother people," I said. "The worst spider is the Australian funnel web spider. Its fangs are so strong they can pierce bone."

crunch!

Mary Grace shuddered. "Creepy!" she said.

"They're not creepy!" I said. "They live underground. They line their burrows with silk and sleep through the winter."

Mary Grace was not impressed. "Dumb old spiders!"

"What do you know? You're just a dumb old girl. A dumb old, stupid, ugly girl."

Mary Grace's eyes got squinty. "I'm telling," she said.

"What'd you say that for, Spider?" Andrew asked as Mary Grace marched over to the sandbox. "Now you'll have to sit on the bench at snack recess."

Ms. Mirabella had strict rules about name-calling.

"You're always talking before you think," Zachary said.

No name-calling!

"I know," I said glumly. "With Mary Grace, I just can't help it."

•

"Diane's thinking about asking her mailman over for dinner," Mom said a few days later. She and Dad were putting plates in the dishwasher.

The Brennermans are divorced. Mary Grace is always bragging about visiting her dad in Florida and getting to go to Disneyworld.

"That's nice," Dad said.

"She asked me for my recipe for *zuppa di lenticchie e riso*," Mom said.

That is soup with rice and other stuff in it.

"Lucky mailman," Dad said, laughing.

"She's so much fun to hang around with," Mom said.

"One of us will say something in the shower, and the next thing you know we've been talking for half an hour."

•

"Mrs. Brennerman takes showers?" Zachary shrieked the next day at recess. "With your mom?"

I nodded miserably.

"And goes on dates?" Andrew asked.

"With a mailman," I said.

"Man," Zachary said. He tossed a piece of tanbark high in the air and tried to stand so that it would land in his shirt pocket. "Does Mrs. Brennerman ever say stuff about Mary Grace?"

"What kind of stuff?"

"I don't know. About when she was a baby. Good stuff. Embarrassing stuff," Zachary said. His eyes glittered. "Stuff we could use."

"I don't think so." I sighed. "It should be against the law for moms of boys to be friends with moms of girls."

"I wonder what Mrs. Brennerman

knows about *you*, Spider," Andrew
said. "I wonder if she tells Mary Grace
embarrassing stuff she's heard about
you."

I had never thought of that before.
My mother can be a big talker. She
loves to tell about when I was four
and read the Park Theater sign back-
wards. And about the time I talked
Louise into gluing her hands to the
kitchen table.

"Why did you have to go and
wonder a thing like that?" I asked.

3

Carpooling

The next week, my mom and Mrs. Brennerman started carpooling. In the mornings, my mom drove Louise and Mary Grace and me to school. Louise and Mary Grace sat next to each other in the back seat and talked about whose moms let them wear nail polish and who did the best cartwheels.

When we pulled into the parking

lot, I scrunched down low and hoped
no one would notice Mary Grace
getting out of my mom's car.

The afternoons were awful. Louise
went to the library to study, so Mary
Grace and I waited alone at the edge
of the parking lot for Mrs. Brennner-
man to pick us up. I did handstands
and pretended to be interested in the
notices on the bulletin board. Anything so that no one would know
I was waiting with Mary Grace.

The worst thing was that I had to
sit in the back seat between Mary
Grace and her little sister, Angel.
Angel hated her car seat. She was
always trying to unbuckle herself
when she thought no one was looking.
Sometimes when she got really mad,
she threw her bottle of apple juice

on the floor and waited for Mrs. Brennerman to twist around and pick it up.

I tried not to think about how my
legs were touching the same seat as
Mary Grace's. Sometimes when you
try not to think about something,
though, you think about it even
harder.

If Angel didn't scream too much,
Mrs. Brennerman would try to talk to
me. I could tell she wanted to make
me feel comfortable. She asked me
things like what I liked best about
school and who my friends were and
did I play sports. When I told her
about liking spiders, she told me about
how Little Miss Muffet was a real kid
whose father made her eat mashed-up
spiders when she was sick.

No matter how much I liked Mrs.

Brennerman, I still didn't want her to be friends with my mom. I started trying to think of things that Mrs. Brennerman wouldn't like about my mom. It was hard. My mom is a pretty nice person. She would make a good friend.

In the car on Tuesday, Mary Grace said, "I got a hundred percent on my spelling test."

"Good for you, honey," Mrs. Brennerman said.

"Did *you* get a hundred percent?" Mary Grace asked me. Even though she already knew. I never get a hundred percent on anything.

"I missed four," I said.

"Good job," Mrs. Brennerman said, to be nice. Then she asked me how my

Inuit report was coming along.

"Okay," I said.

"I finished mine," Mary Grace said. "I'm making a papier-mâché mask for extra credit." Mary Grace always does things for extra credit.

"I'm still working on the writing part. It's really hard for me to write neatly," I said. "Messy writing runs in my family."

"Is that so?" Mrs. Brennerman said.

"Yeah," I said. "You should see my mom's writing. Boy, is it messy! Her *t*'s are too tall. She always forgets to close her *o*'s."

"Oh, my," Mrs. Brennerman said.

Ms. Mirabella told us that neat handwriting makes a good impression. Mrs. Brennerman would definitely not want to be friends with someone who forgets to close her *o*'s.

I felt a little bit bad because my mom's handwriting isn't all that messy. But then I thought about her telling Mrs. Brennerman what I looked like with pureed peas smeared all over my face. And Mrs. Brennerman telling Mary Grace.
I felt a little better.

"The funniest thing I ever saw was my dad pretending to be scared on 'The Pirates of the Caribbean' at Disneyworld," Mary Grace said on Wednesday. Girls always think stupid things are funny.

"The funniest thing I ever saw was my mom singing 'Meet the Flintstones'

and burping at the same time,"
I said.

In the rearview mirror,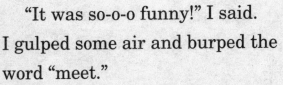
Mrs. Brennerman's
forehead got all crinkly.
"What?" she said, as
though she didn't believe
me.

"It was so-o-o funny!" I said.

I gulped some air and burped the
word "meet."

But before I could show her how
the rest of the song sounded, Mrs.
Brennerman put up her hand like a
policeman at an intersection. "Thank
you, Joey," she said. "I believe I get
the picture."

Mary Grace sat as far away from
me as she could without unbuckling
her seat belt. "You are so disgusting,

Joey Storch," she said.

That ought to do it, I thought.
If there's one thing moms hate, it's
burping.

4

Brown-Pea Soup

"I invited Diane over for dinner next weekend," Mom said that night. I almost fell into my ravioli.

"Great," Dad said. "Why not this weekend?"

"She's cooking dinner for Frank the mailman," Mom said.

"Hmm," I said, but I was not really thinking about mailmen. I was imagining Mrs. Brennerman sitting in our living room. What if Mom brought out my baby album? What if she showed the video of my first swimming lesson?

Then I thought of something. "Hey!

What about Mary Grace?"

"Oh, she's coming, too—
and Angel."

"Mom!"

"It's not the end of the world, Joey."

"It is, too," I said. "I wish I was
dead. I wish Mary Grace was dead."

"Joseph Wolfgang Storch," Mom
said. "You mind your manners."

My mom calls me by my whole
name when she is shocked at how
rude I am. I don't mean to be rude.

I just talk before I think, like Zachary
says.

"I'm not playing with her," I said,
folding my arms hard across my chest.

"Louise will play with her. You can
just be nice to her," Mom said. She
gave me a look. "It won't kill you to
be nice. Besides, you might find something about her to like. You never
 know."

"There isn't anything to like,"
I said, but Mom had already stopped
paying attention to me.

"That reminds me," she said as she
helped Dad clear the table. "I've got
to get my recipe for *zuppa di lenticchie
e riso* to Diane." She looked at me and
smiled. She had already forgotten
about calling me Joseph Wolfgang
Storch. "Will you give it to her

tomorrow on the way home from
school, Joey?"

"Okay," I said. "I hope nobody sees
me with a recipe," I added.

"Thanks, honey," Mom said. She
leaned down and kissed the top of my
head.

I wondered whether Mom would be
kissing my head if she knew that I'd
told Mrs. Brennerman that she liked
to burp and sing at the same time.

"Are you sure Mrs. Brennerman
wants to come here for dinner?"
I asked.

"Why wouldn't she?"
Mom asked. "Unless she
thinks I'm going to poison
her roast beef," she added,
laughing.

Zachary and Andrew and I met behind the auditorium before school. I handed paper and a pencil to Zachary. Of all of us, Zachary had the most grown-up handwriting.

I took Mom's recipe out of my pocket and read the list of ingredients. There were things like onions and tomatoes and lentils.

"What are lentils?" Andrew asked.

"They're like peas," I said. "Only brown."

"Gross," Andrew said.

"I like soup that just plops out of a can," Zachary said.

"Now what kinds of really disgusting stuff can we put in this recipe?" I asked.

"Yeah. How can we really ruin Mrs. Brennerman's soup?" Zachary asked.

"How can you ruin something with brown peas in it?" Andrew asked. "It's already ruined."

Like third grade, I thought. Suddenly I was furious. "It was bad enough just being in the same class with Mary Grace. Now she's going to come to my house and see my baby pictures and touch all my stuff."

Zachary and Andrew nodded. I could tell that they understood.

"It stinks," I said. I didn't care anymore about liking Mrs. Brennerman. I was desperate. I had to do something.

5

Sugarlips

In the end, I gave Mrs. Brennerman a recipe for *zuppa di lenticchie e
riso* that was almost like the one my
mom gave to me. Except for the two
cups of catsup, the three cups of
cinnamon, and the fish heads, it was
exactly the same.

"Why, thank you, Joey," she said
when I handed her the piece of paper

with the recipe copied on it. She put it in her purse without reading it. "I'll bet this is just delicious!"

She really did have a pretty smile.

•

"What's everybody doing this weekend?" Ms. Mirabella asked on Friday.

Travis Hoffberg was going to the aquarium. Regina Littlefield was going to wait for her grandma to come out of surgery. Zachary's uncle was taking him to the movies.

Mary Grace raised her hand. "This weekend my mom's having dinner with the mailman," she said. "Next weekend, I'm having dinner at Joey's house."

I couldn't believe she said it. I couldn't believe she could be so stupid.

But Mary Grace is like that. She is so busy explaining everything that sometimes she just forgets to shut up.

I sunk low in my chair. I wished the roof of the school would cave in.

"I'm sure you'll have a lovely time. I hear Joey's mother is quite a cook," Ms. Mirabella said. She looked around the room sternly. "No giggling, class."

Everyone stopped giggling right away. Ms. Mirabella never had to say anything twice. But that didn't mean it was over.

I knew about giggling. I knew it wasn't over.

•

"Mary Grace and Joey, sitting in a tree, k-i-s-s-i-n-g," Regina Littlefield sang at recess.

"Shut up, Regina!" I yelled.

"Ooh! He's defending his true love!" Regina yelled back. She scrunched up her lips and blew me a kiss.

"Listen, Regina," Mary Grace said. "I do *not* love Joey Storch! If there is one person I do not love, it is Joey Storch!"

"Then how come you're going to his house for dinner?" Regina asked.

"Because my mother and his mother are friends," Mary Grace said.

"That means they hang out together. Which means..." Regina stuck her pointy finger at me and smiled a huge, goofy smile, "*you* hang out together!"

"As a matter of fact, I'm not even going to be there!" I said.

"Oh, sure," Regina said.

"I'm not. I'm going to the circus with my grandfather. Who's a lion tamer." I had a feeling I might be talking without thinking again.

Regina just laughed. Mary Grace shook her head and turned away.

"We have front-row seats!" I yelled.

"Like I'd believe anything you'd

say," Regina said. She batted her
eyelashes and held her hands over her
heart and looked at me in a moony,
goopy way.

Regina Littlefield was the
best spitter in third grade. I'd
always pretended not to
notice, but secretly I thought it
was cool.

It was hard to believe that anyone
who could spit as well as Regina
Littlefield could be so crummy.

The third-grade girls started calling
me Loverboy. Everywhere I went I
could hear them making big, smacky
kissing sounds and giggling. Then

Jeremy Bettencourt, who is in the fourth grade and who my father says is a juvenile delinquent, decided that I looked more like a Sugarlips than a Loverboy.

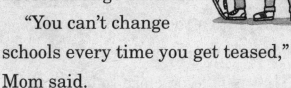

When the fourth-grade boys started calling me Sugarlips, I asked my mom if I could change schools.

"You can't change schools every time you get teased," Mom said.

"Why not?" I asked. "There are a million schools around. Why can't I just go to a new one?"

Mom put down her checkbook and closed her eyes. "Because the new one will have fourth-grade boys, too," she said. She stuffed a check into an envelope and licked it closed. "You have to find another way to handle your problems, honey," she said.

"You don't know what it's like being called Sugarlips!" I cried.

"When I was in the second grade, Agnes Brewster said I smelled like cat food," Mom said. "Every time I walked into a room, all the girls would mew."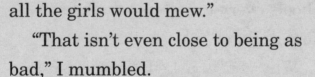

"That isn't even close to being as bad," I mumbled.

"It was no picnic, let me tell you," Mom said.

I was quiet for a while. "So what did you do, anyway?" I finally asked.

Mom shrugged. "Played Barbies

with Eleanor Forbes and tried not to think about it," she said. "Then one day Eleanor told Agnes that she smelled like cough syrup. By the next day, everyone had stopped mewing." She smiled. "Agnes wouldn't ride the bus for a month after that. It was amazing."

"I guess," I said. But I was thinking that it was sure easy to shut up second-grade girls.

And that I wouldn't be in this mess if Mrs. Brennerman's kid was a boy.

6

Spider's Plan

We met behind the trees next to the sandbox. "What did you bring?" I asked.

"Glue, honey, and pancake syrup," Zachary said.

"Molasses, cottage cheese, and part of Clementine's furball," Andrew said.

"Great," I said. "I brought some of my oatmeal from breakfast. And half a tube of suntan oil. And a bowl and a spoon to mix everything up in. And these." I pulled some rubber spiders out of my jacket pocket.

"I still think real spiders would be better," Zachary said. "Girls hate real spiders."

"I don't want them getting hurt. The spiders, I mean. Anyway, girls hate rubber spiders almost as much as real ones," I said.

We dumped all the jars and baggies out of our backpacks onto the grass. Then we were quiet for a minute.

"This is the worst thing we have ever done," I said. "If we get caught—"

I wanted to warn them. I didn't want them to think it would be easy.

Tee hee!

"It will be worth it," Andrew said, "to see the look on Regina Littlefield's face."

By the time we'd finished mixing everything, we only had about ten minutes left before school started. Zachary kept watch at the end of the hall. Andrew waited outside the classroom while I opened the door and tiptoed in.

I dumped some of the mixture in their desks. Then I smeared it on the seats of their chairs. Then I dipped their pencils and scissors in it and set them back in their pencil boxes.

I finished with only a minute to spare.

At first nobody noticed anything. Everyone was talking and laughing and hanging up their backpacks and putting their homework in the home-work basket.

The next thing I knew, Mary Grace yelled that there was something awful dripping down her legs and that there were spiders crawling into her socks. Regina Littlefield yelled that only babies were afraid of rubber spiders and that it was all my fault. Andrew yelled for Mary Grace to shut up. Zachary yelled that how could I be in love with Mary Grace if I had done something so horrible to her. Ms. Mirabella yelled for everyone to please stop yelling.

In between all the yelling, I thought, how can Regina be such a good spitter and be so cool about spiders when Mary Grace is so crummy? I also thought, boy, are we going to get it.

•

We had to wait outside the principal's office a long time. The principal makes you wait longer when she is going to do something really terrible to you.

I whispered, "Thanks."

Andrew shrugged. "It was nothing." He smiled. "It was fun."

"Yeah," Zachary said. "What are friends for?"

7

What Are Friends For?

Grace and Regina came into the
office to call their moms for clean
clothes. Regina pretended not to see
us, but Mary Grace stared right at me.

"Boy, are you in trouble," she said.

"They might even throw you out of the school."

"They will not." I hoped I sounded brave. Actually, I was worried.

"They can't throw you out of the school unless you do something really bad," Zachary said.

"Yeah," Andrew said. "Like paint bad words on the walls, or kill someone."

"Whatever they do, it'll go on your record. You can never be a crossing guard or get into college," Mary Grace said.

"How do you know?" I asked. My heart sank. I'd always wanted to be a crossing guard.

"I just know," Mary
Grace said.

We sat without talking.
I looked out the window
and saw Mrs. Brenner-
man walking across the
parking lot. She had a
shopping bag in one hand.
Angel was asleep in a
pack on her back.

"Joey smeared sticky stuff all over
my desk," Mary Grace said the second
her mom opened the office door.

I had a feeling that Mary Grace
had already told her mom this on the
phone. But Mary Grace is the kind
of kid who likes to tell grownups the
bad news twice.

Mrs. Brennerman handed Mary
Grace the shopping bag. "Here's some

clean stuff, honey." I thought she might give me a dirty look or ask me why I was being so crummy, but she didn't. She really was a nice lady.

Suddenly I knew what I had to do. Actually, I knew the minute Zachary said, "What are friends for?"

Friends are for having fun with. And for telling things to. Friends make you less afraid when bad things happen.

Spiders don't have friends. If you put two spiders in a cage, they'll try to kill each other. Spiders *like* being lonely.

Moms shouldn't have to live like spiders.

"Can I talk to you alone?" I asked Mrs. Brennerman.

Mrs. Trent, the secretary, said I could go out in the hall.

"I'm coming, too," Mary Grace said, like she thought I was going to tell her mom a whole bunch of lies about her. I started to argue with her, but finally I just gave up. I was too tired and miserable to fight. Besides, I had stuff to say to Mary Grace anyway.

Out in the hall, I turned to face Mary Grace. "I'm sorry about ruining your clothes and all your stuff," I said.

Mary Grace crossed her arms hard and stared at the floor.

"I did it for both of us, you know,"

I said. "So they would think we hated each other and quit teasing us."

"Who's teasing you?" Mrs. Brenner-man asked.

"Everybody," Mary Grace and I said together. Mary Grace smiled a little bit; we never said the same thing at the same time. She still wouldn't look away from the floor, though.

"They call me Loverboy and Sugarlips," I said.

"They say he's my boyfriend," Mary Grace said. "They say we sit under the bleachers and kiss and drink milk and try to get it to come out of our noses."

I did that once during lunch period in second grade. Even the sixth graders had clapped and cheered.

I felt a little bit sorry for Mary Grace, though. I had a feeling that she wasn't the kind of girl who wanted to get a reputation around school for getting milk to run out of her nose.

"For heaven's sake!" Mrs. Brenner-man said. "Why would anybody say those things?"

"Because of you and Mrs. Storch being friends," Mary Grace said quietly.

"Because of Mary Grace coming over to my house next Saturday," I said.

"I see," Mrs. Brennerman said.

The hall was very quiet. I could tell that Mrs. Brennerman was thinking.

"Would you like us to go out to dinner instead of to each other's houses? Just by ourselves," she finally asked.

"Yeah, and also to quit carpooling," Mary Grace said.

"I don't know," Mrs. Brennerman said. "I'll have to talk to Joey's mom about that."

Mary Grace smiled, like everything was all settled.

I wished I felt like smiling. "Um...I have to tell you something," I said to Mrs. Brennerman.

"Sure, Joey," she said. "What is it?"

I took a deep breath and watched
my stomach fill up with air. Then
I looked at Mrs. Brennerman. "I need
my mom's recipe back."

"Oh?"

From the way that she said it,
I could tell that Mrs. Brennerman had
already read the recipe.

"It's not right," I said. "It's not the
one she told me to give to you. It's not
what she wrote down."

Mrs. Brennerman wrinkled up her
forehead as if she were confused.

"Fish heads?"

"I kind of made that up."

"Why, Joey?"

I took another breath. "I thought
that if my mom's recipe messed up
your dinner with Frank the mailman,

then you wouldn't like her anymore
and you wouldn't want to be her
friend."

"But, Joey," Mrs. Brennerman said,
"I like your mom just for who she is.
Not because she's a good cook."

I felt awful. "My mom doesn't
actually sing and burp at the same
time," I said. "Actually, she really
hates that."

"That's a relief." Mrs.
Brennerman smiled.
"May I also take it that
your mom's handwriting
is perfectly adequate?"

I wasn't sure what
"adequate" meant, but I had a feeling.

"She closes her *o*'s and everything,"
I said.

Mrs. Brennerman nodded.

"It's all right about you coming
to my house for dinner. And bringing
Mary Grace." I looked at Mary Grace.
"You can play with Louise. I won't
even come out of my room," I said.
"Just don't tell the whole class you're
coming over."

Mary Grace smiled a little.

"Okay," she said.

I was surprised. Mary Grace
never agreed to do anything I said.

"And I don't mind about carpooling," I said. "It helps my mom
not to have to drive so much."

Mrs. Brennerman looked like
she was thinking again. "How about
if I pick you up at the dry cleaner's
around the corner?" she asked.

Kids didn't hang out at the dry
cleaner's.

"That would be good," I said.

I still think it should be against the law for moms of boys to be friends with moms of girls. But Mrs. Brennerman is pretty cool. Maybe there's hope for Mary Grace.

Probably not. But you never know.